SADDLEBACK Classics

P9-BYJ-231

The Three Musketeers

ALEXANDRE DUMAS

ADAPTED BY

Janice L. Greene

SADDLEBACK
PUBLISHING · INC.

15358

SADDLEBACK Classics

The Count of Monte Cristo
Gulliver's Travels
The Hound of the Baskervilles
The Jungle Book
The Last of the Mohicans
Oliver Twist
The Prince and the Pauper
The Three Musketeers

Development and Production: Laurel Associates, Inc.
Cover and Interior Art: Black Eagle Productions

SADDLEBACK PUBLISHING, INC.
Three Watson
Irvine, CA 92618-2767

Website: www.sdlback.com

ISBN 1-56254-297-4

Printed in the United States of America
05   9 8 7 6 5 4 3 2 1

CONTENTS

1 Meeting the Musketeers

In April of 1625, a young man dressed in rough country clothes set off on the road to Paris. He had a long dark face, a hooked nose, and intelligent eyes. There were only a few gold coins in his pocket. But the 18-year-old had an air of confidence about him. Perhaps that was because he was from Gascony—a part of France where the people are known to be brave and stubborn. The young man's name was D'Artagnan.

D'Artagnan's father, who had been a brave soldier, had given his son an important letter to take to Paris. It was an introduction to Monsieur de Tréville, the captain of King Louis XIII's musketeers.

"The musketeers are the king's favorites," his father had told him. "They are feared by even the cardinal—who fears very little. Go to Monsieur de Tréville with this letter, and he will help you."

Besides the letter and the few gold coins,

D'Artagnan's father had given him a horse. It was an old beast, with a yellowish coat. Its tail was nearly hairless. But no one dared to smile at the animal, for D'Artagnan's eyes were fierce and his sword was sharp. No one smiled, that is, until D'Artagnan stopped at an inn in the town of Meung.

D'Artagnan had just stepped off his horse when he realized that someone was laughing at it. The snickering stranger was a nobleman, with black hair and piercing eyes. Two friends were at his side, laughing along with him.

"You there!" D'Artagnan called to the stranger. "Tell me what you're laughing at, so we can laugh together."

The smiling stranger calmly walked up to him. D'Artagnan noticed there was a scar on the man's temple. The stranger sneered, "Why, that horse is the color of a sweet little buttercup. Or at least it must have been that color when it was young."

"You laugh at the horse because you're afraid to laugh at the master!" D'Artagnan cried, furious at the insult. He drew his sword.

The stranger called out to his two friends. They attacked D'Artagnan with a stick and a shovel. The young man tried to fight them off, but a sharp blow

to his forehead knocked him out.

When D'Artagnan opened his eyes, he was inside the inn, and his head was wrapped in bandages. Looking out the window, he saw that a carriage had pulled up in front of the inn. A young woman was leaning out the window. She was talking to the stranger with the scarred face. The woman was about 20 years old, and very beautiful. Her skin was pale and fine. Her curly blond hair hung down to her shoulders.

"So Cardinal Richelieu has ordered me to—" D'Artagnan heard her say.

"To go back to England immediately, Milady," the stranger interrupted. "If the duke leaves London, you must tell the cardinal right away."

"Aren't you going to punish that rude boy first?" Milady asked.

D'Artagnan had just then rushed out the door. "*That boy* will punish *you*!" he cried.

The stranger put his hand to his sword.

"No!" Milady cried. "There is no time. The smallest delay could mean disaster!"

"You're right," the stranger agreed as he leaped on his horse and rode off.

D'Artagnan ran after him. "*Coward!*" he cried. Then he fainted in the middle of the street.

At five o'clock the next morning, D'Artagnan woke up. His letter to M. de Tréville was missing! He flew into a rage. He threatened to smash everything in the inn if his letter was not found.

The innkeeper said, "It must have been that gentleman who was here yesterday! I'm willing to bet he's the one who stole your letter."

D'Artagnan agreed. There was nothing to do now but leave the inn and continue his journey. He rode on to Paris, sold his yellow horse, and eagerly went to meet M. de Tréville—without his letter.

As usual, the courtyard around M. de Tréville's house was filled with 50 or 60 musketeers. They were loud and playful men who seemed ready for anything.

D'Artagnan made his way to the door. He gave his name to a servant, who told him to wait. Looking around, D'Artagnan noticed a tall, proud musketeer the others called Porthos. Everyone was admiring his shoulder belt. It was embroidered with gold thread and shone like water in sunlight. With Porthos was a man named Aramis. Aramis was a handsome man with dark, gentle eyes and cheeks as soft as a peach.

At last the servant appeared and told D'Artagnan to come into the study. M. de Tréville greeted the young man politely. Then he excused himself, stepped out of the room, and called out angrily, "Athos! Porthos! Aramis!"

When Porthos and Aramis walked in, M. de Tréville burst out, "Do you know what the cardinal told me last night? He said that six of you were fighting in a tavern and six of his guards arrested you. It's humiliating! The cardinal's guards would *never* let themselves get arrested!"

Porthos and Aramis were shaking with rage. "It's true that there were six of us against six of them, sir," Porthos hastily explained. "But they took us off guard—before we had time to draw our swords! Two musketeers were killed, and Athos was wounded. But we didn't surrender! They dragged us away by force."

"And I killed one of them with his own sword," Aramis boasted.

"I didn't know all that," said Tréville. "The cardinal must have been exaggerating."

Just then the door opened. A handsome but horribly pale face peeked into the room.

"*Athos!*" cried Tréville and the musketeers.

"I was just telling these gentlemen that I forbid you to risk your lives needlessly," Tréville said. "The king values brave men like you."

Athos smiled. But then, overcome with pain, he fell unconscious to the floor.

"Bring a doctor!" cried Tréville. "The best one you can find! Hurry! Athos may be dying!"

Luckily, a doctor was already in the house. Aramis and Porthos quickly carried Athos to a quieter room where the doctor could examine him. A short time later, the doctor came out and assured them that Athos' condition was not serious. He had only fainted from loss of blood.

At that the musketeers left, and Tréville turned again to D'Artagnan. "Please excuse me, young man," he said. "I still have very fond memories of your father. What can I do for his son?"

"I planned to ask you to take me into the musketeers," D'Artagnan explained. "But from what I've seen in the last two hours, I realize what an enormous favor that would be to ask of you. I'm afraid I may not deserve it."

Tréville looked thoughtful. "A young man does not become a musketeer overnight," he said. "But the Royal Academy is a good place to start. I'll write a letter to the director, and tomorrow you'll join free of charge. You're a proud fellow, I can see. But don't refuse this little favor."

"I'm sorry I don't have the letter my father wrote to you," D'Artagnan said. "It was stolen from me." He told Tréville what had happened at Meung.

"Did that man have a scar on his temple?" Tréville asked curiously.

"Why, yes!" said D'Artagnan. "Tell me who he is and I'll ask nothing more of you! My revenge comes before anything else!"

"Give up all thought of it, young man!" Tréville advised. "It would be foolish to collide with such a rock. You'd be broken to pieces. And now, I'll write that letter for you."

Tréville went to his desk and began writing the letter to the Academy. D'Artagnan, who had nothing better to do, stared out the window.

Then suddenly his face turned red with anger, and he dashed toward the door. "He won't get away from me this time!" he shouted.

"Who?" asked Tréville.

"The coward who robbed me!" D'Artagnan called back over his shoulder.

And with that, he disappeared.

2 A Reward for D'Artagnan

D'Artagnan raced toward the stairs. But just then, a musketeer stepped out of a door in the hallway. D'Artagnan collided with him, and the man howled in pain. It was Athos—and D'Artagnan had banged into his wounded shoulder.

"Excuse me, but I'm in a hurry," said D'Artagnan without stopping.

Athos grabbed him. "*You're* in a hurry? You're not polite, sir."

"Surely you're not going to give me a lesson in good manners!" D'Artagnan said. "If I weren't running after someone—"

"You can find *me* without running after me. Do you understand?" Athos said coolly.

D'Artagnan understood perfectly. Athos had challenged him to a duel. "Yes," he said. "Where?"

"Near the Carmes-Deschaux monastery. At noon," Athos said.

"I'll be there," said D'Artagnan. Then off he ran as if the devil were at his heels.

At the front door, Porthos was talking with a soldier. As D'Artagnan tried to pass between them, the wind blew Porthos' cloak in front of him. He became tangled in it. When D'Artagnan opened his eyes, he found himself behind Porthos, his nose against the man's shoulder belt.

He was surprised to see that the belt was golden only in front. In back, it was ordinary leather. The vain Porthos had been keeping the leather half covered with his cloak!

"Do you always forget to open your eyes when you run?" Porthos shouted.

"No, I always keep them open," D'Artagnan said. "Sometimes I see things that others don't see."

Porthos then realized what D'Artagnan had seen. His temper flared. "Watch yourself! You'll get yourself thrashed, sir, if you go running into musketeers like that!"

"*Thrashed?* That's a harsh word, sir."

"A man who looks his enemies in the face isn't afraid to use harsh words!" Porthos snapped.

D'Artagnan could not stop teasing Porthos about his half-golden shoulder belt. "I'm sure *you* never turn your back on anyone!" Then he ran off, laughing. Porthos started after him.

"Later!" D'Artagnan called out over his shoulder.

"Then we will meet at one o'clock," Porthos shouted, "behind the Luxembourg palace."

By the time D'Artagnan ran into the street, the man with the scar had disappeared. As his anger cooled, D'Artagnan began to feel bad about angering Porthos and Athos. So when he saw Aramis standing up ahead, he made a vow to be especially polite.

Aramis was talking with two of the king's guards. As D'Artagnan came nearer, he noticed that Aramis had dropped a handkerchief.

D'Artagnan picked it up. "Your handkerchief, sir," he said, handing it over with a flourish.

Aramis' face turned red and the king's guards laughed loudly. One of them said, "Ah, I believe I know which woman gave you that."

Aramis swiftly turned to D'Artagnan. "You are mistaken, sir," he said coldly. "The handkerchief is *not* mine."

When the guards left, D'Artagnan spoke softly to Aramis. "I hope you'll excuse me—"

"You were very impolite!" Aramis interrupted angrily. "A lady's reputation has been damaged because of your inteference."

D'Artagnan was confused. "But *you're* the one who dropped it," he said.

"As I said before—it did *not* come from my pocket," Aramis insisted.

"Then you've lied twice," D'Artagnan said flatly.

"If you're going to take that attitude," said Aramis, "I'll have to teach you some manners. Meet me at Monsieur de Tréville's house. Two o'clock."

The two men bowed. It was nearly noon, so

D'Artagnan headed for the Carmes-Deschaux monastery. "It has to be done," he told himself, "but if I'm killed, at least I'll be killed by a musketeer."

Since D'Artagnan knew no one in Paris, he went to duel Athos alone. Usually, when a man fought a duel, he brought friends along with him. These friends, called *seconds,* would make sure that the fight was fair. And they would also carry the sword fighter away if he was wounded.

D'Artagnan was surprised to see that Athos was alone, too. "I wonder what can be keeping those seconds of mine. . . ." Athos said. "Ah, here they come now."

Athos' seconds were Porthos and Aramis!

Porthos stared at D'Artagnan. "What . . . Why . . . Who . . . ," he stuttered in confusion.

Athos pointed to D'Artagnan and said, "This is the gentleman I have a duel with."

"But *I* have a duel with him, too!" said Porthos.

"But not until one o'clock," said D'Artagnan.

"And *I* have a duel with him," said Aramis.

"But not until two o'clock," said D'Artagnan. "Monsieur Athos has the right to kill me first. And now, Monsieur, on guard!" He drew his sword.

Athos drew his sword. But just then, a group of

men appeared at the corner of the monastery.

"Look! It's the cardinal's guards!" cried Porthos. "Put away your swords!"

But it was too late. The guards walked toward them. "Stop in the name of Cardinal Richelieu!" their leader cried. "You men know that the law forbids dueling. I'm afraid you'll have to come along with us."

Athos recognized the guard who had wounded him. He quickly whispered to the musketeers, "There are five of them, and only three of us. I'm ready to die if you are. I swear I'll never face our captain again after losing a battle."

Athos, Porthos, and Aramis stood shoulder to shoulder. The Cardinal's guards lined up, facing them.

D'Artagnan made up his mind in an instant. He had to choose between the king and the cardinal. King Louis XIII may have been ruler of France, but everyone knew that Cardinal Richelieu was more powerful. D'Artagnan did not hesitate. He turned to Aramis and said, "You're mistaken, sir. It seems there are *four* of us!"

The battle was furious. D'Artagnan fought like a tiger. He ran his sword through the leader of the guards. Then he rushed over to help Athos, who was still weak from his wounds. With D'Artagnan's help, Athos killed the very man who had wounded him earlier. Aramis killed the guard he fought with. After that, only Porthos' opponent was left. But the guard was too brave to surrender to the four men. Bravery is always respected, even in an enemy. The musketeers saluted him and let him go.

D'Artagnan and the musketeers picked up the swords of the cardinal's guards and headed toward Tréville's house. They walked along arm in arm, calling out to every musketeer they met. In their good company, D'Artagnan felt drunk with happiness.

The king was delighted when he learned that his musketeers had defeated the cardinal's guards. When he was told that D'Artagnan had joined the fight and fought very bravely, he gave the young man a handful of gold coins.

D'Artagnan divided the money among his three friends. Porthos objected. He told D'Artagnan he should hire a servant with his share. He even found a man named Planchet for D'Artagnan. Porthos had seen Planchet on a bridge. He was spitting into the water and watching the rings it made. For some reason, Porthos felt that this was a sign of a deep thinker. So he had hired Planchet on the spot.

But the musketeers' money did not last long. Soon all four were penniless. D'Artagnan was thinking about this problem when there was a knock at the door. It was his landlord, a fat, gray-haired fellow named Bonacieux.

"I've heard you are very brave," said Monsieur Bonacieux. "I've come to ask your help. My wife's been kidnapped."

3 All for One, One for All

"*Kidnapped?*" D'Artagnan cried.

"Yes," said Bonacieux. "My wife is the queen's linen maid. I'm sure one of the cardinal's guards kidnapped her to find out what she knows."

"Ah," said D'Artagnan.

"My wife is one of the few people the queen can still trust," Bonacieux explained. "The queen is very much afraid. The cardinal has been worse than ever lately. He will do *anything* to get the queen in trouble."

"Is she in trouble?" asked D'Artagnan.

"The cardinal knows she is in love with the Duke of Buckingham," said Bonacieux. "A letter has been sent to the duke. I think it's some sort of trap to lure him back to Paris."

"Just who do you think kidnapped your wife?" D'Artagnan asked.

"I don't know his name," said Bonacieux, "but

my wife pointed out a frightening man one day. He had a scar on his temple—"

D'Artagnan interrupted, " . . . and piercing eyes, a dark face, black hair—it's my man at Meung!"

"*Your* man?" Bonacieux said in surprise.

"Never mind," said D'Artagnan. "If your man is mine, your revenge will also be mine. I'll kill two birds with one stone. What's the matter?"

"Look, there!" said Bonacieux. "In that doorway across the street."

"*It's my man!*" D'Artagnan and Bonacieux said at the same time. D'Artagnan rushed out the door. He searched for the stranger for half an hour—but it was no use. He had disappeared as if by magic!

When D'Artagnan returned to his apartment, Athos, Porthos, and Aramis were waiting for him. He told them what had happened to Madame Bonacieux.

As D'Artagnan finished his story, Bonacieux ran back into the room, followed by four of the cardinal's guards. "Save me, gentlemen!" he cried.

Porthos and Aramis drew their swords, but D'Artagnan stopped them. He whispered to Bonacieux, "We can't save you unless we stay free. Don't say a word about me, my friends, or the queen. If you do, you'll put us all in prison." He called to the guards, "Take him away!"

When the guards left with their prisoner, D'Artagnan said, "And now, gentlemen, we're going to war with the cardinal. From now on, our motto shall be *All for one, one for all*."

Bonacieux's house was turned into what the police called a mousetrap. Everyone who came to the house was arrested and questioned by the cardinal's men. D'Artagnan's apartment was above Bonacieux's, so he stayed at home and listened constantly. He even removed part of his floor so that only a single layer of wood lay between him and the room below.

The day after Bonacieux's arrest, D'Artagnan heard cries coming from below. The voice sounded like a woman's!

"But I live here!" D'Artagnan heard the woman cry out. "I am Madame Bonacieux!"

"Then you're just the person we've been waiting for," said one of the men.

D'Artagnan dropped out of his window and burst into the room below. Four men were there, but only one was armed. The others attacked D'Artagnan with a chair, a stool, and a large pot. In

10 minutes, D'Artagnan had them all running.

D'Artagnan was now alone with Constance Bonacieux. She sat in a chair, only half conscious. He saw that she was in her early twenties, with dark hair, blue eyes, and a slightly turned-up nose.

When she opened her eyes, she saw that she was alone with her rescuer. She held out her hands to him and smiled. D'Artagnan's heart beat faster. He thought Madame Bonacieux had the most charming smile in the world.

"Ah, it was you who saved me, sir!" she cried. "Let me thank you."

"I did only what any other gentleman would have done," said D'Artagnan.

"You're too modest," she said with a warm smile. "But why isn't my husband here?"

"He was arrested and taken to prison—to the Bastille," D'Artagnan explained.

"The *Bastille!*" cried Madame Bonacieux. "What has he done?" Then, strangely, a smile mixed with the look of fear on her face.

"I think he was arrested because he is your husband, madame," said D'Artagnan. "I know why you were kidnapped. But how did you escape?"

"When they left me alone for a little while, I tied

my sheets together and climbed out the window," she explained. "I came here as soon as I could. I thought my husband would be here."

"So he could protect you?" asked D'Artagnan.

"I wanted him to find the queen's valet for me. I must know what's happened in the palace during the last three days."

"I can find the valet for you," said D'Artagnan.

"It's not that simple," said Madame Bonacieux. She looked at him closely for a moment. "If I gave you a password, would you promise to forget it as soon as you said it?" she asked.

"Yes—on my word of honor!" said D'Artagnan.

She whispered the secret phrase to D'Artagnan. Then she said, "These words will get you inside the Louvre. When you get there, tell the valet that I have to see him at once."

D'Artagnan took Madame Bonacieux to Athos' house, where she would be safe. When he said goodbye, he gave her a long, loving look. Then he went to the Louvre, spoke the secret password, and met the queen's valet. He told him where Madame Bonacieux was hiding.

Now that his job was finished, D'Artagnan set off for home. As he walked, he looked up at the stars, sometimes sighing and sometimes smiling. He was thinking about Madame Bonacieux.

He was still thinking of Constance Bonacieux when he saw a woman who looked very much like her. She was walking down the street with a man in a musketeer's uniform. The man was carefully holding a handkerchief over his face.

D'Artagnan followed them. He was certain that the woman was Madame Bonacieux—and the man looked like Aramis! D'Artagnan's heart boiled over with suspicion and jealousy. He felt betrayed by his friend and the woman he already loved.

D'Artagnan ran past them and turned to block their path.

In a tone of annoyance, the man said, "What do you want, sir?" His accent was foreign.

"You're not Aramis?" said D'Artagnan.

"No, sir," he said. "Let me pass, since I'm not the man you thought I was."

"That's true, sir," said D'Artagnan. "But I do want to speak to this lady."

"Please," said Madame Bonacieux.

"Take my arm, madame," the foreigner said, "and let's be on our way."

As the man tried to push the young musketeer

aside, D'Artagnan leaped back and drew his sword. But the foreigner drew his own sword with lightning speed.

"In the name of heaven, Your Grace!" Madame Bonacieux cried out in alarm. She stepped between the two men and took hold of their swords, one in each hand.

"Your *Grace?*" cried D'Artagnan in confusion. "Excuse me, but are you—"

"He's the Duke of Buckingham," whispered Madame Bonacieux, "and now that you know it, our fate depends on you."

"Forgive me," said D'Artagnan, turning to the duke. "I love her, Your Grace, and I'm afraid I was jealous. Please tell me how I can serve you—even at the risk of my life!"

"You're a fine young man," said Buckingham as he shook D'Artagnan's hand. "I accept your offer. Follow twenty steps behind us until we reach the Louvre. If anyone spies on us, kill him!"

D'Artagnan obediently put his sword under his arm and followed Madame Bonacieux and the duke. They reached the Louvre without any trouble.

4 A Spy in the Palace

D'Artagnan left them. Then Madame Bonacieux led the duke along the dark passages of the Louvre. She told him to wait in a small room.

The duke would be killed if anyone found him in the Louvre—but he was never afraid. He had received a letter signed by the queen, asking him to come to France. When he learned later that the letter was forged, he stayed in Paris anyway. He would not leave without seeing his love.

He was 35. People said he was the most handsome and elegant nobleman in all of England *or* France. The duke was the favorite of the King of England, and a wealthy, powerful man.

He looked in the mirror and smiled at himself with pride and hope. Just then he saw her reflection in the mirror. *The queen!*

Queen Anne was about 26. She carried herself like a goddess. Her lovely emerald-green eyes were both soft and majestic at the same time.

"I'm here to see you for the last time," she said sadly. "Everything separates us—the sea, the hate between our two countries, and the vows of my marriage."

"Your words are harsh," said the duke, "but your voice is sweet. Oh, my dearest! You know you are my happiness and my hope."

The duke continued speaking words of love, remembering the last time they met. The queen became more and more nervous as the hour grew late. At last she said, "You must leave, Duke! If you are killed here because of me, my sorrow would drive me mad!"

"Then let me have some small remembrance," the duke said. "Give me something to remind me that this wasn't all a dream."

The queen went to her rooms and quickly returned with a rosewood jewel box.

The duke took it and kissed her hand. "I'll see you again in six months," he said, "even if I have to turn the world upside down to do it!"

Madame Bonacieux led him out of the Louvre as carefully as she had ushered him in.

Meanwhile, Madame Bonacieux's husband was cursing the day he had married her. Bonacieux's character was a mixture of selfishness and greed— with a dash of cowardice to top it off! His love for his young wife was a very small part of him.

In all of his 51 years, Bonacieux had never been so frightened. After he was questioned in the Bastille, the guards took him to another building. They led him to a stuffy room. There, sitting before a fire, was a man of average height with a proud manner. His long, thin face was made still longer by a pointed beard. It was Cardinal Richelieu himself! His body seemed to be weak, although he was still in his twenties. But the power of his fine mind had made him one of the most extraordinary men who ever lived.

After the cardinal questioned Bonacieux for several minutes, he learned two things. First, that Bonacieux was a fool. Second, that the man knew nothing of his wife's secrets. But the cardinal was clever enough to become very friendly with Bonacieux. "It's clear you were arrested by mistake," he said kindly. He held out a bag of gold coins to the greedy man. "Take this, sir, and please forgive me," he said.

When Bonacieux left the room he happily shouted, "Long live the great cardinal!"

A little later, the door opened and a man with a scar stepped inside. D'Artagnan knew him as the man from Meung. He was the Count de Rochefort.

"What have you done with Bonacieux?" Rochefort asked the cardinal.

"I've done the most that could be done," the cardinal said. "From now on, he'll spy on his wife."

"I have news," said Rochefort. "The queen and the duke have seen each other."

"Are you *sure*?" the cardinal demanded.

"Yes," said Rochefort. "We have an excellent spy in the palace. She's learned that the queen gave Buckingham a rosewood jewel box. Inside are the diamond buttons His Majesty gave the queen."

The cardinal sat down and wrote a letter. Then he called for a messenger. "Deliver this letter to Milady in England," he said. "If you come back to me within six days, you'll be paid double in gold."

The letter contained instructions:

Milady:

Go to the next ball the Duke of Buckingham will be attending. The duke will be wearing 12 diamond buttons. Move close to him so you can cut off two of them. Let me know as soon as you have the buttons in hand.

Next the cardinal paid a visit to the king. He suggested that His Majesty plan a ball. It would be a perfect time for the queen to wear the beautiful diamond buttons His Majesty had given her.

When King Louis told the queen about the ball, she turned very pale.

The king did not know just why, but somehow he enjoyed seeing her fear. One of the bad sides of his nature was a taste for cruelty.

"When will the ball be held?" asked the queen.

"Soon," said the king. "I don't remember the exact date. I'll ask the cardinal."

"Then the *cardinal* suggested the ball?" the queen asked suspiciously.

"Yes—why do you ask?" answered the king.

"And he was the one who suggested I wear the diamond buttons?" said the queen.

"Well, what of it?" the king asked crossly. "You'll come to the ball, won't you?"

"Yes, sire."

"Good. I'll expect you to be there."

The queen curtsied. This was not because of good manners. Her shaking knees were about to give way under her!

When the king left the room, the queen began

to sob. *Of course* the cardinal was behind this! Ever since she had refused the cardinal's love, he had been her enemy.

The situation was desperate. Buckingham had gone back to England. The queen suspected that one of her ladies must be a spy—but she did not know who. There was no one she could count on.

Madame Bonacieux had been hiding in a small room next door. She had heard everything. Now she ran to the queen and said, "Don't be afraid, Your Majesty. I think I have found a way out of your . . . difficulties."

"Look me in the eye," the queen said coldly. "I'm betrayed on all sides. How can I trust you?"

"Your Majesty, I *swear* there is no one more loyal to you than I am! There's a way to save you. We must get the diamond buttons back. You must send a messenger to the duke in England."

"But who can we trust?" the queen asked in a worried voice. "If the messenger is caught, I could be divorced and exiled!"

"I swear he won't be!" Madame Bonacieux promised. If anyone could make this dangerous journey, it was the bold and brave D'Artagnan.

5 Cardinal Richelieu's Plot

D'Artagnan requested a two-week leave from Monsieur Tréville. His three comrades, of course, would come with him.

At two o'clock in the morning, D'Artagnan and his friends rode through the gates of Paris. Their servants followed, armed to the teeth.

All went well until they stopped at Chantilly for breakfast. There, Porthos got in an argument when a man insisted that the cardinal was the true ruler of France. Enraged, Porthos drew his sword.

"Kill that traitor and catch up to us as soon as you can," Athos told Porthos.

The rest of the group rode off. "One down," Athos said to his companions.

Later that day they came across a group of men working on the road. The men seemed to be doing nothing but making muddy holes. Because Aramis did not like to get his boots dirty, he scolded them.

Then the workmen started making fun of the travelers, and a fight broke out. Aramis was quickly wounded and so was Porthos' servant.

"It's an ambush!" shouted D'Artagnan. "Don't fight back! Let's go!"

They rode on, but before long Aramis became too weak to travel. D'Artagnan and Athos had to leave their friend and his servant at an inn.

At midnight, they stopped to rest at Amiens. The jovial innkeeper there seemed to be the most honest, decent man in the world.

"I don't like the innkeeper's face," D'Artagnan whispered suspiciously. "He's *too* friendly." They decided to have Athos' servant guard the horses.

Sure enough, at four o'clock, there was an uproar in the stables. When Athos looked out the window, he saw his servant lying unconscious. Clearly, the poor man had been hit on the head.

They decided to leave as soon as possible. But when Athos went to pay the bill, he had a nasty surprise. The innkeeper said, "This money of yours is counterfeit!"

"You liar!" roared Athos. "I'll cut off your ears!"

But just then, four armed men came through the side doors and rushed at him.

"I'm trapped!" Athos shouted at the top of his lungs. "Go, D'Artagnan! Hurry on your way!"

D'Artagnan and Planchet were still alone when they reached the port of Calais. They found a ship headed for England—and just in time! Before they were a mile from shore, D'Artagnan saw the flash of a cannon shot. The harbor had been closed by order of the cardinal.

At half past 10 the next day, D'Artagnan set foot on English soil. He and Planchet rented horses and set off in search of the duke. D'Artagnan did not speak a word of English, so he wrote the duke's name on a piece of paper. People along the road pointed him in the right direction.

Before long, D'Artagnan was being led into the Duke of Buckingham's elegant house. The duke looked sad when he heard that D'Artagnan had come for the diamond buttons. "I swore I would be buried with them," he said. "But if the queen wants them back—may her will be done."

He opened the rosewood box and took out a length of blue ribbon sparkling with diamonds. He began kissing the diamonds, one by one. Then suddenly he cried out, "How can this be? Two of the buttons are missing! Only ten of them are here!"

"What? Do you think they were stolen?" D'Artagnan asked suspiciously.

"Yes, and I'm sure the cardinal was behind it!" Buckingham cried bitterly. "Look—the ribbon that held them in place has been cut."

"Think, sir. Is there anyone you suspect?" asked D'Artagnan.

"Ah, I do remember something now!" said Buckingham. "A strange thing happened the last time I wore the buttons. Lady de Winter seemed to forget we were on bad terms. She was friendly—*very* friendly. I know that she works for the cardinal—now, when is the king's ball going to take place?"

"Next Monday."

"So, we have just five days to act," the duke said worriedly.

He called his secretary and gave an order—no ships would be allowed to leave England.

"But what will King Charles say to this, Your Grace?" the secretary asked.

"Tell the king I've decided on war. This is my first blow against France," cried the duke.

When the secretary left, Buckingham turned to D'Artagnan. There was a look of relief on his face. "Now we don't have to worry," he said. "The missing buttons won't reach France before you do."

D'Artagnan was truly shocked. He stared at Buckingham in amazement. The king had given him complete power—and he used it to serve his love!

As if he was reading D'Artagnan's thoughts, Buckingham said, "Anne is my true queen. A word from her and I'd betray my country, my king, and even my God!"

That very afternoon, the duke's jeweler was brought to his house. In secret, the jeweler and his men worked day and night. Two days later, the buttons were finished. Not even the duke could see the difference between the queen's old buttons and the new ones.

D'Artagnan and the duke said goodbye. Buckingham arranged for a ship to take D'Artagnan to a small fishing village in France. There, at the village inn, a fine horse was waiting for D'Artagnan. Twelve hours later, he was in Paris.

The following night, King Louis' ball took place. The cardinal noticed the queen was not wearing her diamond buttons. He smiled and told the king.

The king was angry with the queen. "I gave them to you because I wanted you to wear them!"

"Don't be angry, sire! I can have them brought

from the Louvre right away," the queen assured him. She bowed and went to her dressing room.

The cardinal went to the king and handed him a box. Inside were two diamond buttons. "When the queen wears her diamond buttons," he said, "count them. If there are only ten, ask her who could have stolen these two."

Just then the queen appeared. The diamond buttons sparkled on the shoulders of her ballgown. The dancing began. Every time the queen came close to the king, he tried to count the buttons—but there was never enough time! The cardinal's forehead was covered with cold sweat.

At last, the king was able to dance alone with his queen. "Madame," he said, "I believe that two of your diamond buttons are missing. I've brought them to you." He held out the two buttons the cardinal had given him.

"You're giving me two *more*, sire?" said the young queen, pretending to be surprised. "Why, thank you! Now I have fourteen!"

Surprised, the king counted the buttons on her shoulder. There were 12! He called the cardinal to him. "What does this mean?" he demanded sternly.

"It means, sire, that I wanted to give Her Majesty those two buttons," the cardinal said. "But I did not dare to give them myself."

"And I'm very grateful, Cardinal," the queen said with a smile, "because I'm sure these two buttons cost you as much as the other twelve cost His Majesty."

She bowed to the two men and walked away to her dressing room.

D'Artagnan, meanwhile, had been standing nearby. He had seen everything. When the queen went to her dressing room, he felt a tap on his shoulder. It was Constance Bonacieux.

She led him through empty corridors to a dark

room and whispered to him to wait. Then she disappeared through a door that was hidden behind a curtain.

Behind the curtain was a large, well-lit room. D'Artagnan could hear women's voices inside. Several times he heard "Your Majesty." He knew he was next to the queen's dressing room.

Suddenly a lovely hand and arm came through an opening in the curtain. D'Artagnan realized that this was his reward. He fell to his knees and pressed his lips to the hand. Then the queen's fingers gently pulled away, leaving something in his hand. It was a diamond ring! D'Artagnan put it on his finger.

A few minutes later, Madame Bonacieux came through the door. "You must leave now!" she whispered urgently.

"But, my dear—when will I see you again?" D'Artagnan asked in an eager voice.

"I'll send you a note," she whispered, pushing him out of the room. The bold D'Artagnan obeyed like a child—which proves that he was really in love.

6 D'Artagnan Meets Milady

When D'Artagnan arrived home, a note from Constance Bonacieux was waiting for him. She asked him to meet her at a house in Saint-Cloud that night. D'Artagnan hurried to meet her, his heart hammering with joy. But she never appeared. An old man there told him what had happened. Before D'Artagnan had arrived, three men forced Madame Bonacieux into a carriage and drove off. *Kidnapped* again!

D'Artagnan told Monsieur de Tréville about everything that had happened. "This smells of the cardinal," said Tréville. His advice to D'Artagnan was to leave Paris for a while. D'Artagnan agreed. He decided this would be a good time to find out what had happened to his friends.

Porthos was still at the inn at Chantilly. He had been badly wounded in a duel, but he was almost well again. Aramis, too, was recovering from a

wound. D'Artagnan promised his friends that he would return for them and rode off into the night.

D'Artagnan was most worried about Athos. Of all his friends, he cared for Athos the most. There was something *noble* about Athos—and something deeply sad as well.

It turned out that after the fight at the inn, Athos had shut himself up in the cellar. For two weeks he had lived on the inn's hams and sausages, and drunk 150 bottles of wine. He drank several more bottles that night with D'Artagnan. When he was very drunk, he told a strange story.

"My friend was a nobleman, a count," Athos began. "When he was 25, he married a girl of 16. Her beauty was breathtaking. One day when they were out hunting, she was thrown from her horse. While she was lying on the ground, unconscious, the count hurried to loosen her clothes—so she might breathe more easily. He bared her shoulder. You'll never guess what was on it, D'Artagnan!"

"Then tell me," said D'Artagnan.

"The *fleur-de-lis*! The mark of a convicted criminal was branded on her shoulder! The count's angel was a devil! So he tied her hands behind her back and sent her off to be hanged."

Athos buried his face in his hands. Struck with horror, D'Artagnan could only stare at him.

The next morning, Athos told D'Artagnan, "Forget what I said last night. When I drink too much, I tell the most ridiculous stories."

But D'Artagnan could not forget this story.

When Aramis and Porthos were well enough to travel, the four friends returned to Paris. There, a letter for D'Artagnan said that he could now become an official musketeer. This was wonderful news. But D'Artagnan's happiness was not complete—for Madame Bonacieux was still missing.

He had no idea how to find her. However, another woman soon caught his eye. It was Milady, the mysterious woman he had seen in Meung.

D'Artagnan first spotted her in church and then followed her to her house. In her courtyard, he saw her speaking in English to a well-dressed gentleman. D'Artagnan could not understand them—but it was clear that she was angry.

D'Artagnan told the stranger to leave the lady alone, but Milady raised her hand to silence him. "I'd be glad to let you protect me, sir, but this man is my brother-in-law," she said.

The scene might have ended there, but unfortunately the gentleman insulted D'Artagnan. D'Artagnan challenged him to a duel that evening. When the stranger accepted, he told D'Artagnan his name was Lord de Winter.

That evening D'Artagnan and his seconds, the three musketeers, met Lord de Winter.

The battle was over quickly. Athos killed his man with a thrust through the heart. Porthos wounded his opponent. D'Artagnan fought carefully and patiently until Lord de Winter was tired. Then he made a quick move that sent the man's sword flying.

"I'll spare your life for the sake of your sister-in-law," D'Artagnan said.

Lord de Winter was delighted with the young swordsman's mercy. He promised to introduce D'Artagnan to Milady that very evening. D'Artagnan smiled. This is exactly what he had planned.

When Lord de Winter told Milady how D'Artagnan had spared his life, a cloud seemed to pass over her face. Then a strange smile appeared on her lips. D'Artagnan felt uneasy, but Milady's beauty quickly made him forget that feeling. He came back the next day, and the next.

Milady's pretty young maid, a girl named Kitty, looked longingly at D'Artagnan each time he came to visit. One day, she took D'Artagnan aside. "Are you in love with my mistress?" she asked.

"Yes! I'm madly in love with her," he said.

"That's a pity, sir," Kitty said with a frown, "because she doesn't love you at all."

For proof, Kitty showed D'Artagnan a love letter from Milady to the Count de Wardes. When he read it, D'Artagnan turned pale. His vanity was wounded! Then he noticed the way Kitty looked at him. Her eyes were filled with love. D'Artagnan made a plan. He would use Kitty to win Milady's love.

That night, D'Artagnan hid in Kitty's room and listened to her conversation with Milady.

"I *hate* D'Artagnan!" Milady cried. "First he made me lose favor with the cardinal. Then he had Lord de Winter's life in his hands and refused to kill him. That cost me a great deal of money!"

"That's true," said Kitty, "and your son is his uncle's only heir. You would have had control of the fortune until the boy came of age."

"I must take revenge on him!" Milady cried.

The hardness in her voice made D'Artagnan's blood run cold. But when he saw Milady the next day, she was as charming as ever. D'Artagnan no longer liked her—but in spite of himself he was drawn to her as iron is drawn to a magnet.

D'Artagnan had an idea. He wrote a letter telling Milady he would meet her that night at nine o'clock. He signed it "Count de Wardes."

When the hour came, Milady ordered Kitty to put out all the lights. D'Artagnan came into Milady's room, speaking in a whisper. It was a painful night for D'Artagnan. He was with Milady, but her words of love were for another man.

The next day D'Artagnan sent Milady another letter signed with Count de Wardes' name. The letter said that he was too busy to see her again soon. It said she would have to "wait her turn."

Milady was furious. She vowed revenge on the count. She told D'Artagnan she loved him and asked him to prove his love—by killing Count de Wardes. She kissed him. And even though her kiss was cold, he felt drunk with joy. He almost believed Count de Wardes had committed a terrible crime. And he almost believed Milady loved him.

They spent another night together. This time he did not have to pretend. He felt sure of himself. He told her how he had pretended to be the Count de Wardes. He expected a brief storm, followed by tears. But he was terribly mistaken.

Milady turned pale with rage and leaped from the bed. D'Artagnan grabbed the sleeve of her thin negligee. She pulled away from him. The delicate silk tore, baring her shoulder. Her beautiful white shoulder was branded with the fleur-de-lis!

She pulled a gold-handled dagger from a box. "You're going to die!" she screamed.

D'Artagnan snatched up his sword and backed out of the room. Kitty got him out of the house just in time. Milady had rung for her servants and ordered them to kill him.

7 Trading a Life for a Life

After leaving Milady, D'Artagnan went straight to Athos' house. "Milady has a fleur-de-lis branded on her shoulder," D'Artagnan told him.

Athos cried out as if he'd been shot. Milady was the woman he had once married—and sent off to be hanged. Somehow she had survived!

"She's a tigress, a panther!" cried D'Artagnan. "And now I'm the target of her hatred."

"The day after tomorrow, we'll only have men to fear," Athos sighed. "We'll be going to war."

It was true. War had broken out in the south of France. The city of La Rochelle had risen up against the king. Most of La Rochelle was Protestant. The people there did not want Louis XIII, a Catholic, for their ruler.

The fighting at La Rochelle gave England a chance to attack France. The Duke of Buckingham dreamed of beating France and riding into Paris to claim the queen he loved. The cardinal dreamed of beating his rival, Buckingham, and shaming him in the eyes of the same queen.

King Louis sent his army to La Rochelle. Soon the battle became an out-and-out siege. The king's army surrounded the walls of the city. The people inside were trapped. Now the army had only to wait. Soon hunger and fear would force the citizens of La Rochelle to surrender.

It was during this waiting period that the three musketeers crossed paths with the cardinal himself. The musketeers had been out late at an inn. They were riding back to camp when they were stopped by the cardinal and his men.

"I know you," said the cardinal to the three musketeers. "You're not exactly friends of mine, and I'm sorry about that. But I also know you're brave and loyal gentlemen who can be trusted. Do me the honor of coming with me. Then I'll have guards even His Majesty will envy."

The cardinal had the musketeers ride with him to an inn. He told them to wait for him on the ground floor. Then he went upstairs.

Porthos and Aramis sat at a table and began playing dice. Athos paced back and forth, thinking.

As he passed a broken stovepipe, he heard the hum of voices. The stovepipe led to the room above.

Athos signaled to his friends to be quiet. He put his ear to the open end of the pipe.

"Milady," the cardinal was saying, "a small ship will take you to London tomorrow morning. I want you to see Buckingham."

"Let me point out to you," said Milady, "that the duke does not trust me. Ever since the affair with the diamond buttons—"

"But this time you'll come to the duke as my personal messenger," said the cardinal. "Tell him that I know he plans to help La Rochelle. If he does, warn him that I'll ruin the queen."

"Can you carry out that threat?" Milady asked.

"I have a letter he left behind," said the cardinal with a sly smile. "It proves that she's in love with Buckingham, the king's enemy."

"But what if Buckingham refuses to give in?" Milady asked.

"The duke is madly—or stupidly—in love," the cardinal muttered bitterly. "When it's clear that I can destroy the queen's honor, he'll have second thoughts about going to war with us."

"But suppose he *still* refuses," Milady insisted.

"It's not impossible, you know."

"In that case, I'll have to hope for one of those events that change the future of a nation," said the cardinal. "Do you remember how Henry the Fourth died before he could attack Austria?"

"He was assassinated," said Milady.

"Now that I think of it," the cardinal said, "the English Puritans are furious with Buckingham. It's possible that one of them might be willing to rid England of the duke. But I need to find someone clever enough to persuade one of these Puritans."

"You've already found her," said Milady.

"And the Puritan who is ready to die for God's justice?"

"He'll be found," Milady promised him. "And now, will you let me say a few words about *my* enemies? First, there's little Constance Bonacieux."

"But she's in prison," said the cardinal.

"She *was* there," said Milady in a wicked, vengeful voice, "but our good queen had her set free. Now she's hiding in a convent somewhere."

"I can find out where," said the cardinal. "Fear not. I'll soon have an answer for you."

"Good," said Milady. "Now, my most dangerous enemy is D'Artagnan."

"He's a brave young fighter," said the cardinal.

"He made you look foolish in the affair with the diamond buttons!" said Milady. "And now he's sworn to kill me. He knows that I'm the one who had Madame Bonacieux taken away from him. I'll trade you a life for a life. You get rid of this man and I'll get rid of the other."

"I don't know what you mean," said the cardinal, "and I don't want to know. But since I need your help, I'll do as you wish. From what you've told me, this D'Artagnan must be a traitor."

Downstairs, the three musketeers stepped quietly to the back of the room. Now they knew everything they needed to know.

Athos whispered, "Tell the cardinal I've gone ahead as a scout. I'll catch up with you later."

When Porthos and Aramis left with the cardinal, Athos went upstairs to Milady's room. The door was ajar. He stepped inside and bolted the door.

"Who are you?" Milady cried out in surprise. "What do you want?"

When Athos took off his hat and cloak, Milady leaped back as if she had seen a snake. "*Count de La Fere!*" she gasped.

"Yes, Milady," said Athos. "I thought I had killed

you. But it seems the devil has brought you back. He's made you rich and given you another name. But he hasn't wiped away the brand on your body."

Milady's eyes flashed fire. "What do you want?" she said coldly.

"I don't care at all if you have the duke of Buckingham killed," Athos said. "I don't know him. Besides, he's an Englishman. But D'Artagnan is my loyal friend. If you touch one hair on his head, I swear you won't live to commit another crime."

"Monsieur D'Artagnan has cruelly insulted me," Milady snapped. "He must die."

"Is it really *possible* to insult you?" Athos asked.

"He will die," Milady said, "after *she* has died."

Athos felt a rage growing in him like a fever. He drew his pistol and cocked it.

Milady tried to cry out for help, but fear had frozen her tongue.

Athos moved his pistol toward her. The muzzle almost touched her forehead. Then he said calmly, "Give me the letter the cardinal wrote—or I'll put a bullet through your head."

She did not move.

"You have one second to make up your mind," he warned.

The expression on his face told her that he was about to shoot. She reached quickly into her dress and took out a sheet of paper.

"Take it and be damned!" she cried.

Athos went over to the light and read:

The person with this letter has acted under my orders for the good of France.

Richelieu

"You viper!" he hissed. "Now that I've pulled out your fangs, bite if you can."

Athos walked out of the room without looking back. A few hours later, he caught up with his friends. As soon as the cardinal no longer needed them, they set off to find D'Artagnan.

Milady was tempted to tell the cardinal everything. But she was afraid that Athos would tell about her brand. It was better to be silent. She decided to be patient. Once her job for the cardinal was finished, she could take her revenge.

8 As Dangerous as a Viper

As soon as they could, the three musketeers told D'Artagnan of Milady's evil plot. Then the four of them decided to warn the queen and Lord de Winter. After all, Winter was not only Milady's brother-in-law, but Buckingham's friend.

Since they could not leave camp, they sent their servants. Aramis' servant, Bazin, took a letter to the queen. Planchet took a letter to London.

So it happened that when Milady arrived in England, Lord de Winter quickly had her brought to his castle by the sea. There she was taken to a room with bars on the windows.

"You can't do this!" Milady cried out angrily. She was furious with her brother-in-law.

"I'll be leaving soon with the army for La Rochelle," Lord de Winter said. "Before I go, you'll be put on a ship and taken to one of our colonies in the south—where you can't harm anyone." He turned to the young officer beside him and said, "Look well at this woman, John Felton. She's young and beautiful—but she's as dangerous as a snake! I've been a friend and a father to you, John. Swear to me that you'll keep her a prisoner—that you won't be tricked by her."

"I'll do as you wish, sir," Felton promised.

The men left her. Milady burst into a fit of rage. Then she calmed herself. She still had her beauty and her cunning. All was not lost.

The next day, Felton came to her room. "Lord de Winter has allowed you to read your mass every day," he said. He laid the mass book on a table.

Milady heard the scorn in his voice when he said *your mass*. She looked at his haircut. Seeing that the man was a Puritan, she made a plan.

"*My* mass?" she said. "Lord de Winter knows I am not a Catholic. This is one of his traps."

Later that day, she sang hymns that were popular with the Puritans. Her voice was pure and lovely. Her guards stopped and listened as if they had been turned to stone. John Felton thought he was hearing the voice of an angel.

By the third day, Felton was talking to her. She was a Puritan, too, she told him. Like all good

Puritans, she hated the Duke of Buckingham—the godless man the Puritans called Satan.

On the fifth day, she made up a terrible story. She told Felton that Buckingham had kept her captive in his house. When it was clear she would rather die than give in to him, he had branded her.

"Look," cried Milady. She opened her dress and showed him the terrible brand.

Felton covered her hand with kisses. Now he was ready to kill Buckingham—even to die for her!

The next day, she did not see Felton. Instead, Lord de Winter came. He said, "I see you've begun to twist poor Felton's mind. You'll never see him again. Pack your things—we're leaving tomorrow. By then, I'll have a deportation order signed by the Duke of Buckingham."

Milady listened silently.

It stormed that night. Thunder roared like the anger in her soul. Then, suddenly, someone tapped on the window. Felton! He had removed two bars from the window.

She climbed out. Felton was on a rope ladder, high above the ground.

"Put your arms around my neck and don't be afraid," Felton told her.

He slowly climbed down the ladder. Then he stopped short. The sound of the guards' footsteps could be heard below.

"They'll see us!" Milady whispered.

"Not unless there's lightning," said Felton.

The guards passed under them, talking and laughing. Milady fainted with relief. Reaching the ground, he carried her to a small boat. When she opened her eyes, it was early morning and she was onboard a ship. Felton told her that the ship was on its way to the town of Portsmouth, where Buckingham was staying. "Lord de Winter sent me to see the Duke of Buckingham—to give him a paper to sign," Felton explained. "He thinks I don't know what message I carry, but I do. It's your deportation order. And he told me to hurry—for tomorrow the duke plans to attack La Rochelle."

"He must not leave!" cried Milady.

"Don't worry, I'll see that he won't," said Felton confidently. His voice was as strong as iron.

When they reached Portsmouth, Felton said goodbye. But before he left, he and Milady made a plan. She agreed to wait for him onboard the ship until ten o'clock that morning. If he did not join her by then, she would instruct the captain to set sail for France. They would meet again at the French convent of Béthune.

When Felton arrived in Portsmouth at eight o'clock, the whole town was up and about. Drums were beating. The fever of war was in the air. Felton found the building where the duke was staying and showed his servants the paper from Lord de Winter. He was brought to the duke immediately.

When the Duke of Buckingham saw the order, he quickly picked up a pen.

"I beg you not to sign this order," Felton said. "The woman he mentions is truly an angel. You must set her free."

"What are you saying? Why, this woman is a dangerous criminal—a *demon*!" cried Buckingham.

"Look into your heart," Felton begged. "You must do justice to her!"

"You must be mad to speak to me like this!" Buckingham cried.

"Take care, Your Grace!" Felton warned him. "England is tired of your sins! God will surely punish you later—but *I* will punish you today!"

The duke reached for his sword just as Felton took a dagger from his shirt.

A servant came into the room. "Your Grace!

There is important news from France."

Buckingham forgot everything else. As he turned to speak to the servant, Felton stabbed him deep in the side. He turned and ran out of the room as Buckingham slumped to the floor.

The servant called for a doctor. News of the attack spread quickly through the town. The fleeing Felton was captured immediately.

Buckingham was dying. He begged to hear the news from France. He was desperate for any word from his dear Queen Anne. "She told me to tell you that she still loves you," the messenger said.

"Thank God!" Buckingham cried. "Let me give her . . ." He looked around for some precious object. But all he saw was the bloody dagger Felton had dropped. "Give her that knife," he gasped.

A minute later the doctor arrived, but the Duke of Buckingham was already dead.

The guards led Felton from the duke's house. But just then, as he stared out to sea, Felton saw Milady's ship leaving the harbor.

"Please tell me the time," Felton asked.

"Ten minutes to nine," was the answer. Milady had betrayed him.

§9 A Plan of Revenge

As Milady's boat left England, she saw a black flag flying from a warship. She knew what it meant. Buckingham was dead or dying. Another ship set sail soon after Milady's.

Milady arrived at the convent at Béthune early in the morning. She showed the abbess the order from the cardinal. The abbess gave her a room and had breakfast served. After Milady had eaten, the abbess came to visit her.

Was the abbess on the side of the cardinal or the king? Milady did not know. So she started to speak against the cardinal in a mild way. She noticed that the abbess smiled. Then Milady began telling the abbess more about the cruelty the cardinal had shown his enemies.

"One of the young women here has suffered much from the cardinal," said the abbess.

"Maybe I'm going to discover something here,"

Milady thought. "It looks as if I'm in luck."

"I am a victim of the cardinal, too," she said, pretending to look grief-stricken. "That order I gave you actually means that I'm a captive here."

"We'll do everything we can to make your captivity comfortable," the abbess said. "I know you'll like the young woman I mentioned."

Milady was soon introduced to the young woman. The abbess did not give the woman's real name, but Milady discovered it soon enough. Just as before, Milady spoke of her love for the queen and her fear of the cardinal. That opened the innocent young woman's heart to her. She told Milady that she knew some of the musketeers. Milady told the young woman she knew D'Artagnan.

"*D'Artagnan!*" the young woman cried out in surprise. "How do you know him?" Jealousy was plain on her face.

"We're friends!" said Milady. "I know who you are now—you're Madame Bonacieux! D'Artagnan loves you with all his heart."

The women hugged. If Milady's physical strength had been as great as her hatred, she would have crushed Madame Bonacieux.

"Soon I'll be leaving with D'Artagnan," Madame

Bonacieux confided. "He's coming tomorrow."

"Here?" Milady asked in surprise.

They heard hoofbeats approaching the convent. Madame Bonacieux ran eagerly to the window. "Oh!" she cried. "Has he come already?"

But it was a visitor for Milady—the Count de Rochefort. Milady quickly told him about the Duke of Buckingham's death. She also told him that she had discovered Madame Bonacieux.

"What good luck!" Rochefort cried. "The cardinal didn't know where Madame Bonacieux was hiding."

"But D'Artagnan and his friends are coming for her tomorrow," Milady went on. "These musketeers are always working against the cardinal. Why hasn't he put them in prison?"

Rochefort said, "The cardinal has a weakness for those men that I don't understand."

"Well, you can tell him that Madame Bonacieux won't escape him again," Milady said.

"I'll tell him," said Rochefort. "Then he'll decide what you must do next. But for now you must stay hidden—at least until the uproar of Buckingham's murder dies down."

"I must not stay here," Milady said. "My enemies

will be arriving soon. Meet me in Armentiéres."

She wrote *Armentiéres* on a piece of paper so Rochefort wouldn't forget it. For safekeeping, he stuck the paper into the lining of his hat.

Milady and Rochefort said goodbye. Then Rochefort rode off toward Paris to deliver Milady's news to the cardinal.

On the way, he stopped at an inn at Arras for a fresh horse. The four musketeers were also at the inn. They had been at La Rochelle, but had taken a leave of absence. Ever since they learned that Milady was headed for Béthune, D'Artagnan had been worried about Madame Bonacieux.

D'Artagnan had just stepped inside the inn when he turned and saw Rochefort ride past. A gust of wind had lifted his hat. Although Rochefort caught it and quickly pulled it down over his eyes, D'Artagnan had recognized him.

D'Artagnan raced back outside. "It's the man from Meung!" he cried. Athos, Porthos, and Aramis immediately came running.

A stableman was chasing after Rochefort. "Stop, sir!" he cried. "A piece of paper fell out of your hat!"

"I'll pay you well for that piece of paper!" D'Artagnan told him.

"It's yours!" said the stableman.

The four friends bent over the paper. "It's in Milady's handwriting!" Athos cried.

"That settles it, then. Let's hurry to Béthune, gentlemen!" D'Artagnan declared.

* * *

Meanwhile, Milady was planning revenge against D'Artagnan. She had decided to take Madame Bonacieux to a secret cottage in Armentíeres. There she could be used as a hostage if necessary. But as Milady and Madame Bonacieux were having dinner, they heard hoofbeats approaching. Milady looked out the window. The four musketeers were coming!

Milady turned to Madame Bonacieux. "It's the cardinal's men!" she said. "We must escape!"

Madame Bonacieux was frozen with terror. She took two steps and fell to her knees. "I'm too weak," she said. "You must go without me."

Milady ran to the table. From the setting of her ring, she took out a small reddish pellet. She dropped it into a glass of wine.

"Here, drink this. Some wine will give you strength," she said.

As Madame Bonacieux drank, Milady turned and ran from the room.

A few minutes later, the musketeers found Madame Bonacieux. When she saw D'Artagnan, she cried out desperately, "Oh, D'Artagnan, my love! You've come at last! It's really you. I'm so glad I didn't run away with her!"

"*Her?*" D'Artagnan asked.

"Yes," said Madame Bonacieux. "Just a moment. My head feels so strange . . . I can hardly see . . . Yes, dear—Madame de Winter."

The men cried out as Madame Bonacieux slowly crumpled to the floor. Porthos and Aramis caught her. D'Artagnan took her in his arms.

Athos was staring at the wine glass on the table, his face full of horror. "Poor woman," he said in a broken voice.

Porthos called for help at the top of his lungs.

"It's no use," said Athos. "There's no antidote for the poison she uses."

With her last bit of strength, Madame Bonacieux took D'Artagnan's head between her hands and pressed her lips to his.

"Constance! My dear Constance!" he moaned.

A moment later, the beautiful young body grew cold and still in his arms.

Just then, a man appeared in the doorway. He

looked at the dead body of Madame Bonacieux. "Gentlemen," he said, "I believe that you and I are looking for the same woman. She must have been here—because I see a corpse. I am Lord de Winter. My ship left England soon after Madame de Winter's. She was always a step ahead of me. Now I see that I have come too late."

Athos bent over D'Artagnan and held him gently. In shock and grief, D'Artagnan hid his face against Athos' chest. He sobbed pitifully.

"Weep, D'Artagnan," Athos said. "Then we will have our revenge."

"I must be part of this," Lord de Winter insisted. "Lady de Winter is my sister-in-law."

"Yes—but she is *my* wife," Athos said in a small, unhappy voice.

D'Artagnan, Porthos, and Aramis stared. Athos must be sure of his revenge to reveal such a secret!

"Give me the piece of paper that fell out of that man's hat," Athos demanded.

"I understand now!" D'Artagnan cried. "It's the name of the town, written in her hand!"

"You see?" said Athos. "There really is a God in heaven!"

§10 The Sword of Justice

The musketeers were eager to set off after Milady, but Athos told them to wait. He went out alone into the dark, stormy night. Before long he returned with a stranger—a tall, gaunt masked man wearing a big red cloak. Together, they all rode off to find Milady.

Porthos and Lord de Winter tried to talk to the masked man several times. But he would only answer with a bow of his head. They soon found Milady hiding in a little house near the riverbank.

Athos went up to the window and broke it with his knee. Then he leaped into the room. Milady screamed and ran to the door—but D'Artagnan was just outside, waiting there.

As the men surrounded her, Milady understood that there was no escape. She sank into a chair.

"We are going to try you for your crimes," Lord de Winter said. "D'Artagnan is your first accuser."

D'Artagnan stepped forward and said, "I accuse this woman of poisoning Madame Bonacieux, who died last night."

The Lord de Winter stepped forward next. "And I accuse this woman of plotting to have the Duke of Buckingham murdered," he said coldly.

"Now it's my turn," said Athos. "I married this woman. And then one day I discovered that a fleur-de-lis was branded on her shoulder."

Milady leaped to her feet. "But where is your *proof* that I committed any crime?" she cried.

The man in the red cloak stepped forward.

"That's for me to answer," he said solemnly.

"Who is this man?" cried Milady, choking with rage and fear.

The stranger took off his mask. Milady stared in terror at the pale face surrounded by long black hair. She knew who he was. "No! It's the executioner of Lille!" she screamed.

"My dear brother was a young priest," the executioner said. "You led him into a life of crime. When he was convicted, I had to brand him—*my own brother*! Then I tracked you down and branded you, too. But somehow the two of you managed to escape. Later I heard that you had left him and found a new victim—the Count de La Fere."

Everyone in the room looked over at Athos. Now they knew his real name.

The executioner went on, "You and you alone destroyed my brother's honor and happiness. He hanged himself."

"Monsieur D'Artagnan," Athos said sternly, "what sentence do you demand for this woman?"

"Death," said D'Artagnan.

"Death," said the rest.

They took Milady to the River Lys. By now the rain had stopped and the dying moon glowed red.

The executioner tied her hands and feet and carried her to a boat. Her fearful cries tugged at D'Artagnan's heart.

"I can't watch such a horrible thing!" he said. "I can't let her be killed this way!"

Milady was desperate. "D'Artagnan!" she called out. "Remember that I love you!"

D'Artagnan began walking toward her. But Athos drew his sword and stood in front of him.

"If you take one more step, D'Artagnan," Athos warned, "you and I will cross swords."

D'Artagnan fell to his knees and prayed.

"Executioner," said Athos, "do your duty."

Athos, D'Artagnan, Lord de Winter, and the executioner each forgave Milady for her crimes. The executioner picked her up and placed her in the boat. As was the custom, Athos stepped forward and gave the executioner a sum of money. "Here is your fee for the execution," he said. "I want to make it clear that we're acting as judges."

"Very well," said the executioner. "And now I want to make it clear to this woman that *I* am acting only from a sense of duty."

He threw the money in the river.

The boat moved across the river to the opposite

bank. Secretly, Milady was able to slip off the rope that was tied around her ankles. When the boat touched the bank, she leaped out and ran. But she slipped on the wet ground and fell to her knees.

The executioner raised his arms. Pale rays of moonlight shone on the broad blade of his sword. There was one short scream as he brought the blade down on her neck.

The executioner took off his red cloak and spread it on the ground. He put the body and the head on it and wrapped them up. Then he lifted the bloody bundle and carried it back to the little boat.

In the middle of the river, he stopped the boat. He lifted up the cloak-wrapped body and called out loudly, "God's justice be done!"

Then the executioner dropped the body into the river and watched the cold waters close over it.

Three days later, the musketeers returned to Paris. The evening they arrived, they went to visit Monsieur de Tréville.

"Welcome back to Paris, gentlemen," he said. "Did you enjoy your leave?"

"Yes, sir, very much," Athos muttered through gritted teeth.

11 An Officer's Commission

The news of Buckingham's death had just reached Paris. At first, the queen refused to believe it. She was even foolish enough to exclaim, "It's not true! He just wrote to me!"

But the next day she was forced to believe it. A friend came from England carrying Buckingham's last bloody gift to her.

The king was overjoyed with the news. He made a great show of happiness in front of the queen. Like all weak men, Louis XIII was not without a streak of cruelty.

The musketeers rode back to La Rochelle. Their journey was as sad as a funeral march. Then one day, as they stopped at a tavern, D'Artagnan spotted the man from Meung.

D'Artagnan leapt from his chair. "This time you won't escape me!" he cried.

But instead of running off, the man came

forward to meet D'Artagnan. "I'm Count de Rochefort," he said. "I have orders to bring you to the cardinal. You're under arrest."

D'Artagnan was forced to return to Paris. His three friends came with him. They waited anxiously outside the cardinal's house while Rochefort led his prisoner into the study. Then Rochefort left and D'Artagnan faced the cardinal alone.

The cardinal looked at him sternly and said, "You're accused of plotting with France's enemies. The punishment for such a crime is death!"

"And who's accused me of that, sir?" said D'Artagnan. "Lady de Winter? A woman who was branded as a criminal. A woman who married one man in England and another one in France. The murderer of the woman I loved!"

"If she's committed those crimes, she'll be punished," said the cardinal.

"She's already been punished," D'Artagnan said bitterly. He then described the murder of Madame Bonacieux, the trial in the house where Milady was hiding, and the way she was put to death.

The cardinal shuddered. "You men are musketeers, not judges," he said. "You had no right to try this woman and execute her. Now you must go on trial yourself. I can tell you in advance you'll be found guilty."

"Give your orders, sir," D'Artagnan said calmly. "But I do have your pardon in my pocket."

D'Artagnan handed him the paper that Athos had taken from Milady.

The cardinal read: *The person with this letter had acted under my orders, for the good of France.* The note was signed with his own name!

The cardinal was silent. "He's trying to decide how to put me to death," D'Artagnan told himself. "Well, he'll see how a nobleman dies!"

The cardinal looked at D'Artagnan's intelligent young face. He thought of the wit and courage this young man could offer a good master.

He tore up the paper and began writing a letter. When he finished, he handed it to D'Artagnan. "I've left a blank space for your name," he said. "You can write it in yourself."

The letter was a commission as lieutenant of the musketeers! In gratitude, D'Artagnan fell to his knees before the cardinal.

"My friends deserve this much more than I," D'Artagnan cried. "But I will never forget this, sir!"

The cardinal turned and called out, "Rochefort!"

Rochefort came in immediately. "I now count Monsieur D'Artagnan among my friends," the cardinal said. "I want you to embrace each other—and behave yourselves."

Rochefort and D'Artagnan embraced coldly. But as soon as they left the cardinal, Rochefort said, "We'll meet again, won't we?"

"Name the time and place," said D'Artagnan. "I'll be there with my seconds."

Just then the cardinal opened the door behind them and stared at them suspiciously.

"What are you saying?" he asked.

D'Artagnan and Rochefort smiled at each other, shook hands, and bowed to the cardinal.

* * *

D'Artagnan took his commission to Athos. "Take it," he said. "You have every right to it."

Athos smiled and shook his head. "It's too much for Athos and not enough for Count de La Fere. Keep it—it's yours."

Next, D'Artagnan went to see Porthos, who was trying on some very elegant clothes. D'Artagnan offered him the commission. "Write your name on it," D'Artagnan urged his friend, "and treat me well when I'm under your orders."

"No, D'Artagnan. Keep your commission for yourself," Porthos said. "I don't need it. I'm going to be marrying a rich widow soon. I was just trying on my wedding clothes when you came in."

Finally, D'Artagnan went to Aramis. But he, too, refused the commission. "No, my friend," said Aramis. "I'm finally going to become a monk."

D'Artagnan went back to Athos. "They all refused it," he said. Smiling, Athos took a pen and signed D'Artagnan's name to the commission. "No one is more worthy than you," he said.

"Now I'll have no more friends," D'Artagnan cried. "I'll have nothing but bitter memories."

Tears rolled down his cheeks. He let his head fall between his hands.

"You're young," Athos said sympathetically. "Your bitter memories still have time to turn into sweet ones."

Epilogue

Without Buckingham to rescue La Rochelle, the town finally surrendered. The king rode into Paris in triumph—as if he had beaten an enemy instead of his own French citizens.

Porthos married and became a wealthy man.

Aramis became a monk.

Athos continued on as a musketeer under D'Artagnan's command until 1633. Then he quit, saying he had inherited some money.

D'Artagnan fought three duels with Rochefort. He wounded him three times.

"I'll probably kill you the next time," D'Artagnan said, as he helped Rochefort to his feet.

"Then we probably shouldn't fight again," said Rochefort. "I'm more your friend than you know. I could have had you put to death after our first duel. All I had to do was say a word to the cardinal."

The two men then embraced, and this time their

respect and affection was genuine.

Rochefort appointed the faithful Planchet as a sergeant of the guards.

Monsieur Bonacieux lived peacefully for some time. He did not know what had happened to his wife—and he cared very little. Then one day he made a very foolish mistake. He wrote a letter to the cardinal, just to let him know that he was still around. The cardinal wrote back. He said he would take care of him from now on.

Monsieur Bonacieux left home at seven o'clock the next morning. He never returned. Many people said that he was staying in a well-guarded castle, with bars on the windows. They said the generous cardinal was paying for his food and rent.